THE CAR WASHING STREET

DENISE LEWIS PATRICK

pictures by **JOHN WARD**

SCHOLASTIC INC.

New York Toronto London Auckland Sydney

Text copyright © 1993 by Denise Lewis Patrick.
Illustrations copyright © 1993 by John Ward.
All rights reserved. Published by Scholastic Inc., 555 Broadway,
New York, NY 10012, by arrangement with Tambourine Books,
a division of William Morrow & Company, Inc.
The illustrations were painted with acrylic on canvas.
Front cover lettering by Filomena Tuosto.
Printed in the U.S.A.
ISBN 0-590-54349-0

20 19 18   40   07 08 09 10 11

For Matthew
D.L.P.

For Olympia, my anchor to reality
J.W.

It's Saturday morning, and the city is already sticky and hot. On the street where Matthew lives, something interesting is about to happen.

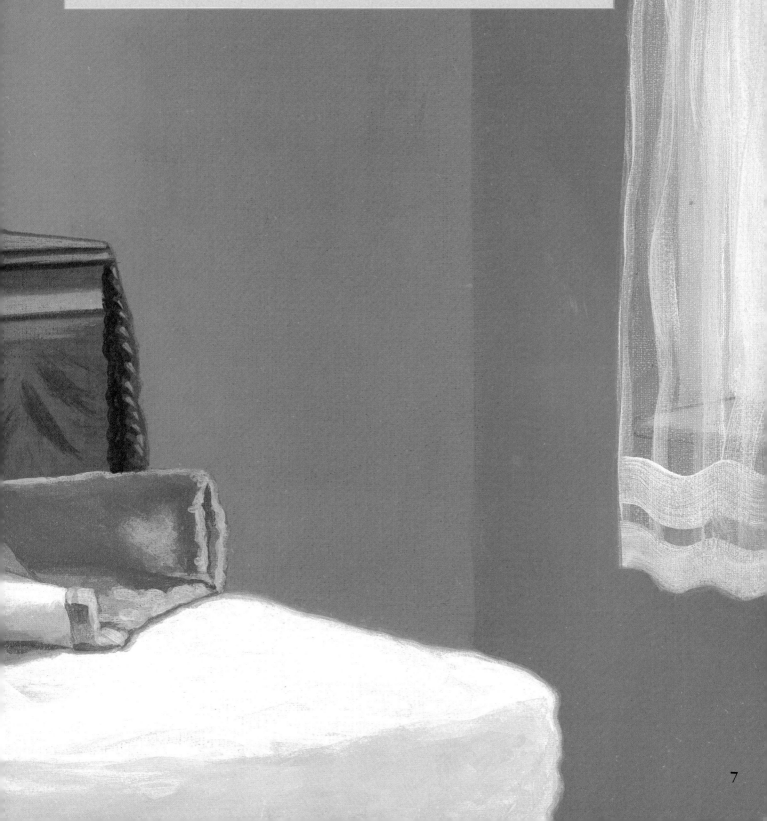

Matthew awakes to a clink-clink-clink! Then he hears water splishing and splashing. When he runs to his window, he sees Mr. Henry Hamilton coming out of his house with a big bucket, a brush, and a bunch of old rags.

"Daddy!" Matthew yells. "Hurry! It's car washing time!"

Matthew's mama and daddy don't have a car, but Matthew loves watching his neighbors wash and rinse and polish theirs. They wash cars all year round, and Matthew is right there every week, watching.

Daddy pours glasses of ice-cold orange juice. As Matthew and Daddy step out the door, they can already hear Junior Boy Taylor's big radio.

Junior Boy bounces out of his apartment building. He's got his radio in one hand and a bright green hose and some big yellow sponges in the other.

Matthew and his daddy sit on the steps in the sun. All along the street people are washing their cars. Mr. Henry Hamilton already has his car soaped up. Junior Boy is still trying to find a good radio station.

Across the street, Mrs. Kennedy is wiping her big pink Cadillac with a little pink towel. Mr. and Mrs. Rodriguez and the Rodriguez kids are throwing water onto their station wagon.

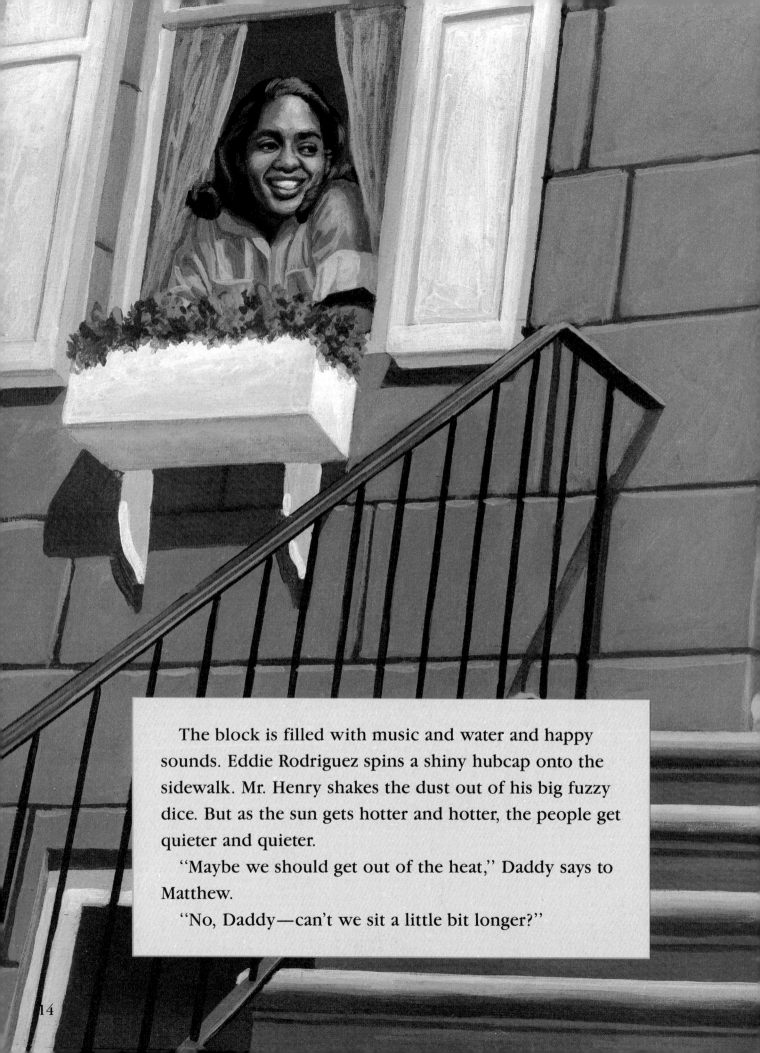

The block is filled with music and water and happy sounds. Eddie Rodriguez spins a shiny hubcap onto the sidewalk. Mr. Henry shakes the dust out of his big fuzzy dice. But as the sun gets hotter and hotter, the people get quieter and quieter.

"Maybe we should get out of the heat," Daddy says to Matthew.

"No, Daddy—can't we sit a little bit longer?"

Just then, Junior Boy's hose wiggles right out of his hands. It flips and flops on the street. Suddenly, Mr. Henry Hamilton's fishing hat is dripping with water.

"Hey!" Mr. Henry shouts.

"Mr. H., I didn't mean it!" says Junior Boy.

Mr. Henry snatches up his bucket. With one swing of his arm, he splashes water back out toward Junior Boy. Junior Boy ducks.

The water flies clear across the street onto Eddie Rodriguez!

"Sorry," yells Mr. Henry Hamilton. But it's too late. Eddie puts his hand over the fire hydrant and shoots a waterfall way up into the air.

"Oooh," Matthew squeals, as the cold water rolls down his face.

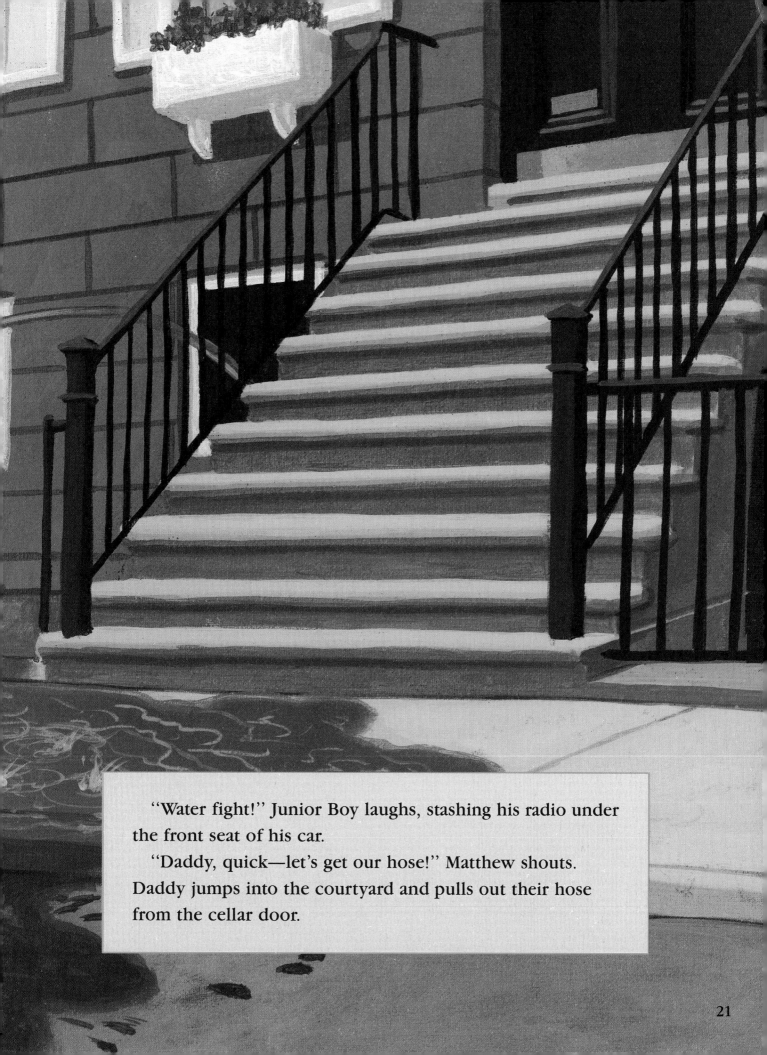

"Water fight!" Junior Boy laughs, stashing his radio under the front seat of his car.

"Daddy, quick—let's get our hose!" Matthew shouts. Daddy jumps into the courtyard and pulls out their hose from the cellar door.

Quick as snap, everyone joins in the fun. Matthew moon-walks under the waterfall. Eddie and Nilda and Georgie Rodriguez start a slippery conga line. Even Mrs. Kennedy hikes up her skirt and prances like a ballet dancer. In a little while, everyone is soggy and soaked and *cool*.

People begin to laugh and talk all at once. Junior Boy turns his radio back on.

"Look!" Matthew points down the street. Miss Emma is coming, pushing her cart with its big rumpled umbrella.

"Ices!" she sings. "I've got coconut, grape, and strawberry iiiicces!" She stops right in front of Matthew's house. The neighbors gather around and crunch into the ices as they dry their faces and arms.

Matthew and his mama and daddy sit on the steps.
The Rodriguezes come over and sit down, too.

"You know," begins Mr. Henry Hamilton, "every time we
set out to wash these cars—"

"Something wild happens!" Junior Boy finishes.

Matthew laughs and says, "That's why I like living on the Car Washing Street."